Brownies

For Hannah, who loved being
a Brownie so much

STRIPES PUBLISHING
An imprint of Magi Publications
1 The Coda Centre, 189 Munster Road,
London SW6 6AW

A paperback original. First published in Great Britain in 2009
Published by arrangement with Girlguiding UK
Brownie logo, uniforms and badges copyright © Girlguiding UK
Text copyright © Caroline Plaisted, 2009. Illustrations copyright © Katie Wood, 2009

ISBN: 978-1-84715-104-9

A CIP catalogue record for this book is available
from the British Library.

Printed and bound in the UK.
2 4 6 8 10 9 7 5 3

Brownies

Friends Forever

Meet the Brownies

Katie

Katie, Grace's twin, is super sporty and likes to play games and win. She wants to get every Brownie badge and her Six is Foxes!

Jamila

Jamila's got too many brothers, so she loves Brownies because NO BOYS ARE ALLOWED! Jamila is a Badger!

Ellie

Awesome at art and crafts, Ellie used to be a Rainbow and likes making new friends. Ellie is a Hedgehog!

Animal-crazy Charlie has a guinea pig called Nibbles. She loves Brownie quizzes and Pow Wows. Her Six is Squirrels!

Charlie

Grace

Grace is Katie's twin sister and she's ballet bonkers. Grace enjoys going on Brownie outings, and she is a Rabbit!

Chapter 1

It was Tuesday – Brownie night! The 1st Badenbridge Brownies were gathering in the hall for a meeting.

"Hey, Jamila! Do you think we're going to make something tonight?" asked Ellie.

Ellie and Jamila had both joined Brownies on the same night, along with their best friends Charlie, and Katie and Grace – who were twins. They all went to the same school, but at Brownies Charlie was a Squirrel, Katie was in the Foxes, Grace was a Rabbit, Jamila was a Badger and Ellie was a Hedgehog.

"I hope so," said Jamila, "and I hope it's something we can eat – I'm starving!"

Every week at Brownies the girls made crafts, played games, did puzzles, or sang songs. Every meeting was different – and that's why they loved Brownies so much!

"Boo!"

Jamila and Ellie turned round. It was Charlie. She'd just arrived with her big sister, Boo, who was the Seconder in the Rabbits.

"Hi!" Jamila smiled.

"Hi!" Charlie grinned back. "Are Katie and Grace here yet? I'm dying to meet her!"

"Meet who?" asked Boo. "Is someone new coming to Brownies tonight?"

"Of course!" Ellie giggled. "Sienna!"

"Oh yeah – Katie and Grace's cousin," said Boo, suddenly remembering.

"How could you forget about her!" Charlie laughed. "She's come all the way from Australia, after all."

"Hey, look," said Jamila excitedly. "They're here!"

Jamila pointed towards the door of the hall. Katie and Grace had just arrived with Sienna. She was wearing a pair of dark-blue culottes and a pale-blue polo shirt under her jacket. It was the first time any of the friends had seen her because she'd only arrived the day before.

Ellie looked puzzled. "I thought Sienna was a Brownie," she said, waving at the three girls as they talked to Vicky and Sam, the Brownie Leaders. "But her clothes don't look like ours. Is she a Guide?"

"She can't be a Guide – she's the same age as us," said Charlie.

"Come on," said Jamila. "The others are all at their Six tables already. We'd better sit down too!"

Soon everyone was in their Sixes, and Sienna joined in with Katie and the rest of the Foxes.

"We're all doing an Alphabet Challenge," Megan, the Squirrels' Sixer, explained to her Six.

"How does it work?" asked Bethany.

"You have to write the alphabet down the left-hand side of the page," said Ashvini, who was the Seconder. "Then you have to find things around the hall with names beginning with each letter."

"Great!" said Charlie, grabbing a piece of paper and a pen and starting to write.

"So that new girl is Katie and Grace's cousin?" asked Megan.

"Yes," said Charlie. "She's Australian!"

"Cool!" chorused all the others.

"Come on," said Megan. "We'd better get on with this challenge or we won't have it finished in time."

Ten minutes later, Sam called out, "Can you finish what you're doing, please, girls, then join us in the Brownie Ring for a Pow Wow."

11

Pow Wows were when the Brownies told their news and suggested ideas for Brownie fun. The girls quickly seated themselves in a circle on the floor, looking eagerly at their Leaders.

"We've got lots of things to do this evening," said Vicky.

"Yes," added Sam, "but first, we've got an introduction to make. I expect you've all noticed we have a new member tonight."

The Brownies all looked at Sienna, who was sitting next to a grinning Katie in the Brownie Ring. The new girl smiled at the others, a bit embarrassed by all the attention.

"This is Sienna," Vicky continued. "She's Katie and Grace's cousin from near Melbourne in Australia."

"Sienna is a member of Girl Guides," said Sam, "and she's going to be coming to our meetings while she's in the UK."

"How come you're wearing different clothes to us?" Ellie asked Sienna.

"This is what I wear for Guides," Sienna explained. Her polo shirt had a picture of a trefoil with the words "Girl Guides Australia" underneath.

"Guides?" said Charlie. "But you're not old enough! Aren't you a Brownie?"

"We don't have Brownies in Australia," said Sienna.

The girls were puzzled. How could they not have Brownies?

"We're all called Guides, whatever our age," Sienna continued.

"Wow!" the Brownies replied.

"So are you going to be here long?" asked Holly, the Badgers' Seconder.

"A few weeks," Sienna explained.

"Come on everyone – let's give Sienna a

special Brownie Welcome," said Sam.

All the girls stood up in the Brownie Ring. First they clapped their hands above their heads, then to their right, and then to their left. Each time the Brownies called out "WELCOME!"

"Thanks!" Sienna said, smiling.

Sienna, an Australian Guide from the 2nd Olave Valley Guides, was now a member of the 1st Badenbridge Brownies too!

Chapter 2

The 1st Badenbridge Brownies sat down again.

"Next we have to congratulate Emma," said Sam. "Now that Jessica has gone to Guides, she is going to be the Sixer for the Foxes! Emma, would you like to come up, please?"

Emma walked over to Sam and Vicky and held her right hand up in the Brownie sign.

"Well done, Emma. Here's your new Sixer badge," said Vicky, handing it to her.

"Yaaay!" cried the Brownies as they clapped.

"We also need to congratulate Amber," continued Sam. "She is going to be the new Seconder of the Foxes."

Amber jumped up and rushed over to the Leaders to collect her badge. She was beaming from ear to ear as the Brownies clapped.

"Now," said Sam, "we've got some other exciting news – all the Badenbridge Brownie and Guide units are going on an outing!"

"Ooooh!" gasped everyone in the room.

"We're all off to Badenbridge Manor the Sunday after next," explained Vicky, "for our annual District outing."

"It's a stately home with lots to explore," said Sam. "There's a letter about it for all of

you to take home. Make sure you remember
to collect one at the end of our meeting.
You'll need to bring the permission slip back
next week."

There was a buzz of excitement around
the hall. An outing and a chance to meet
other Brownies and Guides – the girls could
hardly wait! Then Sam raised her right hand
and the room fell silent again.

"We also need to talk about sunflowers!"
she said.

"You mean the Sunflower Competition?"
Faith asked excitedly.

"That's right!" said Sam. "Every year the
First Badenbridge Brownies and the First
Badenbridge Cubs have a competition to see
who can grow the tallest sunflower."

"And last year one of the Cubs won…"
sighed Caitlin.

"No!" groaned the older girls, remembering their disappointment at losing the year before.

"My brother was the winner," wailed Ashvini, "and he's barely stopped showing off about it since!"

"So are we doing it again this year?" asked Katie, who loved competitions, especially the idea of one where the Brownies might beat the Cubs.

"Absolutely," said Vicky. "And tonight we're going to plant up our winning sunflower seeds!"

The Brownies clapped excitedly.

"OK," said Sam. "I've got some pots, seeds, soil and labels on the table over there. Let's get planting!"

Most of the Brownies raced over to the table, but Jamila, Ellie and Charlie paused

to introduce themselves to Sienna.

"Hi, I'm Jamila. Welcome to England!"

"Thanks," said Sienna. "And you two must be Ellie and Charlie – I've heard lots about you from Katie and Grace."

"Your Guide clothes are really cool," said Ellie. "It's great that you remembered to bring them over with you."

"It was my Guide Leader who said I should," said Sienna. "I hadn't realized I'd be dressed so differently from Katie and Grace."

"It's amazing, isn't it?" said Charlie. "There are Brownies and Guides all over the world, wearing different clothes but still having the same fun!"

The 1st Badenbridge Brownies set to work. First, they had to write their name on a label and stick it on the front of a pot, then fill the pot with soil. Then they made a hole in the soil about two centimetres deep, dropped in two sunflower seeds, and covered them over with some earth.

"What happens next?" Katie asked.

"Well, we've been given permission to put our sunflowers in the tray over by the window at the back of the hall," said Sam.

One by one, the Brownies placed their pots carefully in the tray.

"Don't we need to water them?" asked Amy, the Seconder of the Hedgehogs.

"Absolutely!" said Sam. "I've got a watering can here for you all to use on your pots. Amy – why don't you start?"

"Won't they dry up before next week though?" asked Boo.

"They might do," agreed Vicky. "That's where the girls who go to this school are going to be special Brownies for us."

All the girls who went to Badenbridge Primary liked the sound of being a special Brownie.

"Who comes to this school then?" asked Vicky.

A sea of hands waved back at her.

"We need you to keep an eye on the pots for us, and if they look dry, will you ask if you can water them during your break time, please?"

All the special Brownies, including the five best friends, nodded and grinned.

"Great," said Sam.

"Will the sunflowers have grown by our next Brownie meeting?" asked Lottie, one of the Foxes.

"Not quite that soon," said Sam. "It'll take about three months before we get flowers on the plants."

"That's ages!" Lottie replied, and all the other Brownies sighed.

"I know," agreed Sam, "but we'll be able to plant them outside in the school garden in a few weeks' time. And every week we can

check and see how much they've grown."

"Are the Cubs going to plant their sunflowers in the garden too?" asked Ashvini.

"Yes," said Vicky. "Then we can compare them more easily."

"And see that the Brownie ones are taller!" said Chloe.

"We'll easily win!" Katie said.

"Yesss!" agreed all the Brownies.

"OK," said Sam. "We've done our sunflowers. So ... who wants to play a game?"

"Meee!" shouted every Brownie in the hall.

Vicky laughed. "I want you all to stand in a circle," she said. "Don't stay in your Sixes though – mix yourselves up. We're going to play the Name Game – it'll help Sienna learn everyone's names."

Jamila was given a ball. Then she called out the name of one of the other girls, Molly, and threw her the ball. Molly caught it, called out another Brownie's name, threw it to her, and then sat down. Eventually no one was left standing. The Brownies loved it and got the giggles as they kept dropping the ball and had to chase it round the hall.

When the game was over, Sam called everyone back into the Brownie Ring.

"It's nearly time to finish," she explained.

"Noooo!" sighed all the Brownies.

Grace stuck up her hand.

"Yes, Grace?" Vicky asked.

"I was wondering – remember how we found out about Brownies in Africa for Thinking Day?" she said. "Well, is there any way we could find out about Brownies in other countries as well – like Australia?"

There was a muttering of excitement; the other Brownies thought this was a good idea too.

"That's a great suggestion," said Vicky. "In fact, there's a special Brownie badge called the World guiding badge. Perhaps some of you might like to think about doing that? We can talk more about it next week."

"Well then," said Sam. "That gives me an idea of how we can all say goodnight to each other. Let's sing the 'Make New Friends' song!"

"Everyone hold hands," said Vicky, and all the Brownies sang:

Make new friends but keep the old;
One is silver and the other gold.
A circle's round,
It has no end,
That's how long
I want to be your friend!

"That was great," said Sam. "And now, Izzy is going to read an old Chinese saying for us. We'd like you all to think about this over the next week."

"'If every other person were just like me,'" Izzy said, reading from the special

book the Brownies wrote their thoughts in.
"'What sort of world would our world be?
The smile that you send out returns to you.'"

"Ahhh!" said all the Brownies.

"And just remember, girls," said Vicky,
"that you've got ten million other Brownie
and Guide friends around the world! See you
all next week!"

Chapter 3

Next day, Jamila was talking with Ellie in the playground as they waited for Charlie, Katie and Grace to arrive.

"Sienna seemed really nice," said Ellie.

"Yeah," agreed Jamila. "I can't wait to meet her properly after school!"

"Nor me," agreed Ellie.

Katie and Grace had asked Jamila, Ellie and Charlie to come round for tea that afternoon to get to know Sienna better.

"Hey," said Ellie. "Here's Katie and Grace now!"

The twins raced towards them.

"Hi!" they both said at once.

"Did Sienna enjoy Brownies last night?" Ellie asked.

"What's not to like about Brownies!" Grace exclaimed. "She loved it."

Just then, Charlie arrived.

"Morning! What are you lot talking about?"

"Brownies, of course!" declared Jamila. "And Sienna too!"

"So what's it like having your cousin to stay?" asked Charlie.

"It's like having a sleepover every night!"
Katie said excitedly. "Sienna's sleeping in our
room, you see. And during the day, she's doing
loads of stuff with her mum and dad. Then this
weekend we're all going to London."

"Cool," said Jamila.

"Come on, the bell's about to go!" said
Grace.

The five friends gathered up their things
and headed towards the classroom, ready
to start the school day.

"Do you live in the middle of a desert?" Ellie asked Sienna, as the girls munched on cookies later that afternoon. "I saw a film once about a kangaroo in Australia and it looked dusty and really, really hot!"

Sienna giggled. "I don't live in a desert!" she said. "I live in a town, just like you do."

"You mean it's just like Badenbridge?" Jamila asked, astonished.

"It's a bit bigger, but it's not that different. We're quite close to the beach too."

"Are there sharks?" Charlie gasped.

"Yes," said Sienna, "but I don't know anyone who's been eaten by one! When you go to the beach, you have to follow the rules and swim where the lifeguards tell you to."

"It's so cool that you live near the beach!" said Jamila. "Is Australia really hot?"

"Well, it's a lot warmer in the summer than here!" Sienna laughed. "But we still have winter."

"So do you live in a house on stilts?" Charlie asked. "I read somewhere that Australian houses have to be up high so crocodiles can't walk in the front door."

"There are some places where they have lots of crocs," agreed Sienna, "but my town has ordinary houses on ordinary streets."

"What's your school like?" Charlie wanted to know.

"It's pretty big," said Sienna. "The kids in our primary school go up to Year Seven before they go to High School. It's cool – I like my school."

"Tell us about your best friends," Grace urged.

"I've got two – Kizz and TJ." Sienna grinned. "They both live next door to me – Kizz lives on the right and TJ on the left."

"Wow," said Katie, thinking how the five friends could have even more fun if Charlie, Ellie and Jamila lived next door to her and Grace.

"Kizz and TJ are just the best," Sienna went on. "We go to school and Guides together too."

"What happens at Australian Guides?"

asked Ellie. "Is it the same as our Brownies?"

"Pretty much. We play games and do activities and earn badges," said Sienna, "just like you."

"What sort of badges?" Jamila wanted to know.

"All sorts. My unit took part in the Save the Koala campaign," explained Sienna. "We sold lots of stick-on tattoos to people and managed to raise enough money to foster our own koala for a year!"

"Ahh!" said animal-mad Charlie.

Sienna smiled. "We all got badges for that, and we're going to see if we can raise enough to foster a koala for another year as well."

"Do you have sleepovers?" asked Ellie.

"Sure – and shows and activity days," said Sienna. "We go on outings and we do things

with Guides from other units. Oh – and I got my Junior BP Award a couple of months back too."

"What's that?" asked Grace.

"The Baden-Powell Award. All the Guides do it when they're my age. I had to do twelve challenges," said Sienna. "It was tons of work. We had to learn about the Guide Promise and Law, and do outdoor activities. It took me ages, but I was really pleased I'd done it. Kizz and TJ did it as well. We got a special certificate and everything."

"Wow," said Charlie. "That's amazing. I've only got two badges so far."

"But we've already started the Out and about and Entertainer badges," Katie pointed out. "And Vicky said we could do our World guiding badge too, didn't she?"

"I had to do stuff about guiding around the world for my award," said Sienna. "There was loads of stuff about it on a special website my Leader told me to look at."

"Oh, do you mean WAGGGS? We went on that to find out about Brownies in Africa!" exclaimed Katie. "Remember?"

"Hey, why don't we ask Mum if we can go and search on it now?" said Grace.

And all the girls ran downstairs as fast as they could.

With the help of Katie and Grace's mum, the girls logged on to the WAGGGS website.

"We can click through to other websites for Brownies and Guides all over the world from this page," Ellie pointed out.

"See if you can find Australia!" Grace suggested to Katie, who was sitting on the chair in front of the screen.

"OK…" Katie clicked on a drop-down menu above a big map of the world. In a flash, the screen changed to the website for Girl Guides Australia.

"Hey, Sienna – those girls look like you in your Guide clothes!" said Charlie.

"Cool!" Ellie exclaimed.

"Come on," said Sienna. "I'll show you around the site…"

Chapter 4

The five best friends learned lots of things about Australian Guides from surfing the website with Sienna. They couldn't wait to tell Vicky, Sam and the other Brownies all about their findings, but first it was time for the weekend!

On Saturday, Katie and Grace went with Sienna to London. They had a brilliant time sightseeing, and even visited the Brownie shop near Buckingham Palace and bought Brownie keyrings for their three friends.

Monday flew by and soon it was Tuesday

again, and time for Brownies. As soon as the girls arrived at the hall, they checked on their sunflowers, and were pleased to see that a few of the seedlings were starting to peep through the soil. They then rushed to join the Brownie Ring.

"Does anyone have any news for us?" asked Sam, looking round the Ring.

Five hands shot straight up.

"Ellie – what's your news?"

"Sienna told us all about what she gets up to at Guides in Australia. She's been helping the Save the Koala campaign and recycling corks."

"Why did you need to recycle corks, Sienna?" asked Ashvini.

"There's a shortage of cork in the world and an Australian man realized that most bottle corks were being thrown away once the bottle was opened," Sienna explained.

"We read about it on the Australian Guides website," Katie continued. "The Guides have led the way in making sure that people recycle corks. They get broken up and made into other things."

"That's really interesting," said Sam. "Did you find out anything else, girls?"

Charlie's hand shot up.

"The Australian Guides say a Promise that's really similar to ours!"

"And the Australian Guides do things with WAGGGS too! Their Leaders keep in touch with Brownies and Guides around the world," added Grace.

"Can any of our older Brownies remember what WAGGGS stands for?" Vicky asked, looking round the Brownie Ring.

Molly, the Rabbits' Sixer, put up her hand.

"Please, Vicky – is it something like the World Guiding Association?" she suggested.

"That's very nearly right," said Vicky. "Anyone else have a guess?"

Charlie put up her hand.

"Yes, Charlie?" said Sam.

"Is it the World Association of Girl Guides and Girl Scouts?"

Sam grinned. "That's right. We're all members of it!"

"Last week we talked briefly about the

World guiding badge," said Sam. "Is there anyone here who would like to do it?"

Almost every Brownie in the Ring put up her hand, including Sienna.

"But, Vicky!" said Emma and Lauren, who were two of the older Brownies. "We've already done our World guiding badge."

They pointed to a badge they both had sewn on to their Brownie clothes, showing the Brownie trefoil on a blue background, the symbol of World guiding.

"Of course you have, I'd forgotten," said Vicky. "But if you wanted to do some more work on World guiding you could earn yourselves a second badge! Would you like to do that?"

"Yes, please!" they both said.

"Excellent," said Vicky. "Now, to get your badge you all have to do five things out of the list of challenges in your *Brownie Badge Book*. Perhaps Emma and Lauren can remember what some of them are?"

"I remember I had to learn a Brownie song from another country," Lauren replied. "And I made a picture of the World badge and learned what each part of it represents."

"I also remember making a jigsaw with pictures of the World guiding Centres," said Emma.

"And we cooked something from another country," Lauren added.

"That's right." Vicky smiled. "You don't all have to do the same challenges, though. Take a look at the list and decide which ones you fancy doing."

"But tonight," added Sam, "we thought you might like to do the first challenge all together."

"Yeah!" all the Brownies shouted.

"On your Six tables are pictures of Brownies and Guides from around the world," said Sam. "Daisy has downloaded them from the internet for you."

Daisy was a Badenbridge Guide, but she helped out at Brownies as a Young Leader. She'd been a member of the 1st Badenbridge Brownies when she was younger.

"What each of you needs to do is draw pictures of Brownies and Guides from other countries and then cut them out to make paper dolls," Sam explained. "Make as many as you can and, when you've finished, you can join your dolls together to make your very own friendship circle!"

"Brilliant!" the Brownies declared.

"OK, then, let's get started!" said Vicky.

All around the hall, Brownies were busily drawing, colouring and cutting.

"That's amazing!" said Sukia when she saw Ellie's drawings.

Ellie blushed at the praise; she was really good at art and loved making things, but she always got a little embarrassed when people said nice things about her work.

Meanwhile, over with the Foxes, Sienna was having great fun.

"This is really cool," she said, as she carefully cut out one of the paper dolls.

"It looks just like you!" said Amber, the new Seconder.

"It *is* her!" said Katie, giggling.

"I'm going to do a Brownie from
Pakistan," said Emma.

"And I'm doing one from Switzerland,"
said Lottie.

On the Badgers' table, the girls had all
finished drawing and, instead of each
Brownie in the Six making their own
Brownie friendship circle, they'd decided to
join all their paper dolls together to make
one really big one.

"Holly's giving her Brownie a name. She's writing it on her doll," Jasmine pointed out to the others in the Six. "Look!"

"It's not her name," Holly explained. "It's what a Brownie is called in Poland – a *Zuchy*."

"That's a great idea," said Jamila.

"But where did you find out what they're called?" Chloe wanted to know.

"It's on this sheet," said Daisy, who was sitting at their table helping them. "I found it in one of my old Brownie annuals."

"Cool!" said Izzy, their Sixer. "I'm making a Wolfling – a German Brownie."

Meanwhile, the Rabbits had all decided to draw Canadian Brownies, and were busily colouring in their orange T-shirts and hats.

Over at the Squirrels' table, Megan, their Sixer, had a great idea.

"Why don't we spell the word

BROWNIES out of the names of countries where there are Brownies?" she suggested.

"Brilliant!" declared Ashvini. "Which countries shall we choose?"

Charlie suggested Belgium for the B and Bethany came up with Romania and Oman for the R and the O, but then they all got stuck on the W. It was Vicky who helped them by suggesting Wales. Then, between them, the Squirrels came up with New Zealand for N, India for I, Estonia for E and Sri Lanka for S.

"Fabulous work," said Vicky when she saw what they were doing.

"It's going to be really cool when we've finished!" Ashvini grinned.

Later on, Sam and Vicky called all the girls back into the Ring and got them all to explain the Brownie friendship circles that they'd made.

"Great!" Sam smiled. "So you've started to learn things about other Brownies already?"

"Yessss!" they all replied.

"Good," said Sam. "Before next week, perhaps you could have a think about which other tasks you'd like to complete for your badge work. You need to do four more. You can work in pairs, on your own, or perhaps with your whole Six. It's up to you."

Grace put up her hand.

"I think that Brownies all over the world are just like us!" she exclaimed. "Sienna said that her Guide pack in Australia does lots of the same things we do – singing songs!"

"And making friends!" added Jamila.

"And having adventures," said Charlie.

"That's right," agreed Sam. "Does anyone else have any Brownie friends or relatives in other countries?"

"I have!" said Ashvini. "My cousins live in India, and they go to something like Brownies called Bulbuls."

"Do you think you could bring in a photograph of them in their Brownie outfits?" Vicky asked.

"Sure," said Ashvini. "I'll get Mum to email them."

"That would be great," said Vicky.

Katie shot up her hand.

"Please, Vicky!" she said. "Why don't we send Sienna's Guide unit an email? We could ask questions and make friends with them!"

"You mean like pen pals?" said Sam.

"Yes!" said the Brownies.

"That'd be really cool," agreed Sienna. "I've got Kizz and TJ's email addresses with me. We could send the email to one of them to pass on to my unit."

"We'd be making friends with an entire Guide pack on the other side of the world!" exclaimed Sukia. "That would be brilliant!"

All around the hall, the Brownies were getting excited at the thought of making new friends in another country.

Suddenly, Daisy stood up. "Hey – I think I've just had a totally fantastic idea!"

"What's that?" asked Charlie.

"Mum," she said, turning to Vicky, "why don't we make a little video about the First Badenbridge Brownies? We could film a Brownie meeting and send it to Sienna's Guide unit!"

"D'you know, I think that's a great idea!" said Vicky, smiling.

"Let's do it!" agreed Sam.

The Brownies looked at each other and grinned.

"Why don't you bring the video camera to next week's meeting, Daisy." Sam glanced at her watch. "Now, I need to check I've had everyone's permission slips back for the outing. When I've done that, we can talk about what we're going to be doing at Badenbridge House on Sunday, and then it will nearly be time to go home! So, we'd better get cracking…"

Chapter 5

On Thursday evening, the five friends and Sienna were invited round to Jamila's house.

"I made these for all of us," said Sienna, handing Jamila a big cake tin.

Jamila opened the tin. Inside were lots of little square chocolate-and-coconut-coated cakes. "Ooh, yummy! Chocolate cakes!"

"They're called Lamingtons," Sienna explained. "We make them all the time in Australia."

"So they're like a real Australian cake?" Jamila asked as she took a bite.

Sienna nodded.

"Sometimes we make them at Guides and sell them to raise money for charity."

The room fell silent as the six friends tucked in to the delicious, gooey cakes.

"Will you teach me how to make these?" asked Ellie. "They're great."

"Course," said Sienna. "Hey – you could make them as part of the World guiding badge, for the food bit."

"Great idea!" said Jamila. "Then we'd only have three more challenges left to do!"

"So, apart from making Lamingtons, what else have you been up to? How was London?" asked Charlie. Katie and Grace had been so busy with after-school clubs all week that they hadn't had a chance to fill Charlie, Jamila and Ellie in on what they had got up to the previous weekend.

"It was great!" said Sienna. "We visited Buckingham Palace and Big Ben. Then we went shopping – in fact, we got you all something!"

Grace produced the souvenir Brownie key rings that she, Katie and Sienna had bought at the Brownie shop.

"Wow! Thanks!" said Charlie.

"Yeah," said Ellie. "These are brilliant! I'm going to attach mine to my school bag."

"Good idea," agreed Jamila. "Thanks! So, did you do any more sightseeing in London?"

"Well, we went on a riverboat down the Thames. And we went on this big wheel thing that went up really high so that we could see all across London," Sienna continued.

"You mean the London Eye!" said Jamila. "I went on that with my cousins!"

"Mum, Dad and I are going to visit some other parts of the UK next week, and on Saturday we're having a big family party."

"Yes." Grace grinned. "All our other cousins are coming too."

"So are you going to miss the next Brownie meeting if you're going away?" Charlie asked Sienna.

"I'm afraid so – but I'll be here this weekend, so I'll be coming on the Brownie

outing on Sunday," said Sienna.

"Brilliant!" said Jamila. "And it's going to be our first District outing ever."

"I wonder what Badenbridge Manor will be like," said Ellie.

"My mum's been," said Jamila. "She says it's really grand and there's loads to do there."

"Hey, that reminds me!" Sienna said excitedly. "My mum said she'd take us all bowling before I go home. Fancy coming?"

"You bet!" exclaimed all the others at once before grabbing another delicious Lamington each.

At school the next day, the five best friends checked on their sunflowers. They were pleased to see that the plants were now a couple of

Katie.

centimetres tall. As they watered the seedlings, they chatted about the Brownie film they were going to make.

"Do you think we'll all do something in it?" asked Ellie.

"Well, I expect most of it will be about Brownies doing things together, like our Pow Wows and the games we play," Charlie said.

"And we could show them some of the badges that we've got," said Jamila.

"And the sunflowers too," added Grace.

"Good idea!" said Katie, who was hoping that her sunflower would be the biggest.

"We could also sing some of our Brownie songs!" said Charlie.

"There are masses of things we could do for the film," said Jamila. "Everything we do at Brownies is fun!"

Chapter 6

On Saturday afternoon, Grace, Katie and Sienna had their family party, so Ellie and Jamila went round to Charlie's house.

"I wonder if Sienna's Guide unit will reply to us when we send our email next week," Charlie said, as they sat in her room munching on chocolate biscuits.

"I hope so," said Ellie.

"Do you think they'll send us a film of them too?" Jamila asked.

"That would be cool," said Charlie. "I was thinking it would be brilliant if we could send a parcel of Brownie stuff to Australia too."

"What kind of stuff?" asked Ellie.

"You mean things like badges?" said Jamila.

"Yes – and maybe a Brownie T-shirt…"
Charlie suggested.

"That sounds like a great idea!" said Ellie.

"Let's see what the others think when we
see them tomorrow," said Charlie.

"Agreed!" said Ellie and Jamila at the same
time. "Jinx!"

Sunday dawned bright and warm – a perfect
day for a Brownie outing! Charlie couldn't
wait to get to Badenbridge Manor, or to tell
Sienna, Katie and Grace about her idea of
sending the parcel. As the girls sat on the
coach, she filled them in.

"Brilliant!" Grace said. "And I've just had a
thought. One of the challenges for the World
guiding badge is to send a postcard to a

Brownie in another country. We could all send postcards to Sienna's Guide unit in the parcel!"

Katie nodded in agreement. "Great idea! We should tell Vicky and Sam."

"Maybe not today though," suggested Jamila. "They look a bit busy."

Seconds later, the coach pulled up at Badenbridge Manor and the Brownies tumbled out, eager to get going.

"There are loads of Brownies here already!" said Charlie.

She was right – and there were Guides too. The 2nd and 3rd Badenbridge Brownies had already arrived with the Badenbridge Guide unit. Just behind them another bus, with "Powelton Brownies" on its windscreen, pulled up.

"Wow," said Sienna, gazing up at Badenbridge Manor. "This place is ancient!"

Vicky split the Brownies into two groups. For once the girls didn't have to stay in their Sixes, which meant the five best friends and Sienna could be together. First they toured the house: Ellie's favourite room was the nursery because it was full of amazing toys, while the kitchens and dining room fascinated Jamila, because they were laid out as if a banquet was about to happen. On the dining-room table, an entire feast of pretend food was on display.

"All this food is making me hungry!" Jamila gasped, making her friends giggle.

Outside in the gardens, Charlie enjoyed visiting the Butterfly House, where they all stood and gazed in wonder at the hundreds of gorgeous butterflies as they fluttered around.

"This is awesome!" Sienna exclaimed, as a butterfly landed on her head.

"Come on," said Vicky. "Let's find the maze."

The maze was enormous, with high hedge walls. The Brownies split up into groups of three and set off to find its centre. Katie was in a group with Boo and Emma, and they were the first to reach the middle of the maze and ring the bell to tell everyone they'd arrived.

"There you are!" said Katie when the others finally found them. "We've been ringing this for at least ten minutes!"

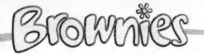

Fortunately, there was a special short cut that led from the centre of the maze back out into the garden, so the Brownies didn't have to retrace their route.

"Hey, look over there!" declared Grace, pointing over to an open-fronted building.

"That's the Barn Theatre," said Sam. "Would you like to go and see it?"

"Would I?" Grace laughed. She was so keen to see it she even beat Katie in the run to reach it. Leaping on to the stage, ballet-mad Grace couldn't resist pirouetting and *jeté*-ing across it.

"Imagine having a theatre in your garden," sighed Sienna. "How cool is that!"

Grace giggled. "If I lived here I'd put on a play every week!"

After a couple of hours, all the different Brownie and Guide units met up for a gigantic picnic on one of the lawns next to the moat that surrounded Badenbridge Manor. What seemed like hundreds of girls munched on their sandwiches, chatted and made new friends. They also had a terrific time singing Brownie and Guide songs at the tops of their voices.

"How amazing is this? What's been your favourite bit of today, Sienna?" Katie asked.

Sienna looked around her, grinned and shrugged. "There's so much that's incredible about this place it's impossible to choose," she said. "I've never been to an old house like

67

this in Australia, and I've never seen so many
Brownies or Guides in one place either…
I haven't got a favourite bit – I love it all!"

Chapter 7

On the coach trip home everyone was talking about what a brilliant time they'd had. All the Brownies agreed that the outing was the best one that the 1st Badenbridge Brownies had ever been on. The following day, Sienna and her parents set off on their sightseeing tour of the UK. The Brownies' meeting on Tuesday felt very strange without her, even though she'd only been with the 1st Badenbridge Brownies for a couple of weeks.

At the beginning of the meeting, the Brownies checked on their sunflowers – some of which had grown even taller since the previous week – then formed a Ring.

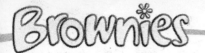

Once Daisy had her video camera set up, ready to film the meeting, Vicky and Sam put up their hands. It took a little while for all the girls to fall silent, but once they had, they sat up very straight, giggling as Daisy pointed her camera around the Ring.

"Hello everyone," said Sam. "We thought we'd write our letter to Sienna's unit in Australia today, so that we can email it off this week. But first, we ought to talk about your World guiding badges and how you are getting on with them. Who'd like to tell us about something they've done this week?"

Ashvini put up her hand. "I sent an email to my cousins in India and they sent back photos of their Bulbuls unit and told me about the things they get up to. They play games just like we do – and they do crafts too! I've made a poster with the photo and

the information they sent. Look!" she said, holding it up for the other Brownies to see.

There was a murmur of approval as everyone saw how hard she had worked.

"That's excellent work," said Vicky. "Well done. What about anyone else?"

Chloe put up her hand and then told the group all about Pax Lodge.

"I went there at the weekend with my family," she explained. "It's a World Centre for Brownies and Girl Guides, and people from all over the world visit it! It's in Hampstead in London, and we stayed there on Saturday night."

"What's a World Centre?" Caitlin asked.

"It's like a home away from home for anyone in the world who is a Brownie or Guide," Chloe explained. "There are four of them – in India, Switzerland, Mexico and London."

"Did you meet any Brownies from other countries?" Holly asked.

"Yes!" Chloe grinned. "There was a really nice Canadian Brownie called Courtney, who was staying there with her mum. There was also this map of the world on the wall in the dining room. Everyone who visits leaves a badge from their unit behind, so I left our unit badge pinned to the map! Courtney left one too. Oh – and we got this special Pax Lodge badge as well."

Chloe showed the new badge that she had on her sash to the others.

"You're only allowed to get this badge if you've visited Pax Lodge," Chloe said proudly.

"That's great, Chloe!" said Sam. "And are you going to keep in touch with Courtney?"

Chloe smiled. "Yes! We're going to be pen pals. I've written a sort of report about my visit to Pax Lodge to show you. I also found out some information about the other three World Centres – see?"

She handed her report to Vicky and Sam.

"Yes, that's fantastic," said Vicky.

"Shall we give Ashvini and Chloe a clap for all their hard work?" said Sam. So the Brownies did, and Daisy filmed all their grinning faces.

"I know that lots of you have been doing things for your badge," said Vicky, "so Sam and I will be coming round to your Six tables later to see how you've been getting on."

"But before we do that," said Sam, "I'm sure you've all noticed that Sienna isn't with us tonight."

"Has she gone back to Australia already?" asked Jasmine, puzzled.

"No, she's just gone on a trip around the UK," explained Katie.

"She'll be back next week for Brownies," Grace added. "But it will be her last week before she does go home."

"No!" sighed all the Brownies, who couldn't believe that their new Brownie friend was going to have to leave so soon.

"It's sad, isn't it?" said Sam. "But don't forget that Sienna will always be our friend –

even if she's on the other side of the world."

"That's right," agreed Vicky, "and we all know that when we want to celebrate with our friends, we have a Brownie party!"

"Yes," Sam continued. "So next week, we'll be having a surprise party for Sienna! I've got some recipes here for Brownie food from around the world that some of you might like to make for the party. The extra good news is that it will count as another task towards your World guiding badge!"

"Cool!" said Ashvini.

"Vicky and I also thought we could make some banners about Sienna and Brownies," said Sam. "What do you think?"

The Brownies couldn't wait to get started and were just about to go to their Six tables when Charlie put up her hand.

"Please, Vicky and Sam! We've had an

idea – well, two ideas actually!"

"Great – tell us all about them!" Vicky replied.

"Well, firstly, Jamila, Ellie, Katie, Sienna, Grace and I thought we could send a parcel of things to the Second Olave Valley Guides in Australia," explained Charlie.

"What sort of things?" Sukia asked.

"Brownie things," said Jamila. "Like our Promise badge."

"And a T-shirt," added Ellie.

"And hopefully the Guides will send us a parcel back!" said Katie.

"And," said Grace, "our second idea was for each of us to write a postcard to Sienna's Guide unit to put in the parcel. We could do it as one of the challenges for our World guiding badge!"

Vicky and Sam grinned at each other.

"You lot always come up with really amazing ideas," said Vicky.

"Has anyone got any other suggestions of what we could put in the parcel?" asked Sam.

One by one, the 1st Badenbridge Brownies came up with things to put in the parcel. Handing the camera over to Vicky, Daisy pulled out the notebook she always carried in her pocket and started to write the ideas down. Jasmine suggested enclosing a set of stamps. Other Brownies thought they could make crafts for the Australian Guides, and include some of the activity sheets and quizzes they did at Brownies.

"I think we've got a really good list of things there," said Sam.

"Yes," agreed Vicky. "We'll come round to your Sixes later on and decide who's going to get which things ready. Now – over to your Six tables and get cracking with those banners for the party!"

All around the room, the Brownies were drawing and painting, and Daisy filmed them as they worked. She got each Brownie to wave at the camera and say their name – most of them got the giggles as they did it!

The Hedgehogs' banner said, "Brownies and Guides are Girls in the Lead". The Rabbits were working on one that said, "We do our best". Meanwhile, the Foxes had decided to make a poster that said, "Brownies and Guides are Helpful!" and the Badgers had designed one that said, "Brownies and Guides Lend a Hand". Finally, the Squirrels decided to make a banner that said, "Farewell, Sienna!" As they worked, Sam and Vicky came round, talking to each girl about their badge work and making suggestions for things that could help them complete their tasks.

As they were finishing, Vicky put up her right hand and soon the room fell silent.

"Your banners are looking great, girls," she said. "They'll make the room look wonderful for Sienna's party. But now we need to write our letter to Australia."

"Yessss!" said all the Brownies.

Daisy carried on filming as the girls tidied up their Six tables and went back into the Brownie Ring to help Vicky and Sam write the letter.

"We could tell them what Badenbridge is like," suggested Jamila.

"And about all the badges we've got!" added Katie.

One by one, the Brownies all made suggestions. They told the Australian Guides all about their Sixes and their badge work. They also wrote about life in Badenbridge and explained about Vicky and Sam being their Leaders and Daisy being a Young Leader. Finally, they told them about Brownie outings they'd been on, especially the trip to Badenbridge Manor.

"OK, girls," said Vicky. "Once Daisy's

finished editing the film, we can send it off with the letter in an email."

"Do you think they'll write back to us by next week?" asked Jamila.

"We'll have to wait and see," said Vicky, "but I'm sure we'll hear from them soon."

"Right, it's almost time to finish," said Sam, "but before we go, does everyone know what they're bringing for the parcel to send to the Second Olave Valley Guides?"

All the girls nodded.

"Great," said Vicky. "And can everyone write a postcard to the Guides in time for next week?"

Everyone nodded again.

"Fantastic!" said Vicky. "What efficient Brownies you are!"

Chapter 8

With Sienna away for only three more days, the five Brownie friends had plenty to do. On Wednesday after school, they met up at Jamila's house to make more decorations for Sienna's farewell party.

Ellie came up with the idea of making posters of koalas and kangaroos to celebrate Sienna being Australian.

"That's brilliant!" said Grace.

The five friends set to work colouring, glittering and stickering their way through the rest of the afternoon. By six o'clock they had a big pile of eye-catching posters.

"They look great, don't they?" said Charlie.

"Fantastic," Jamila agreed. "Hey, we still have to do two more challenges for our World guiding badge. Why don't we each make a poster like the one Ashvini did?"

"Yeah," said Katie. "That was really cool. We could make them all about Australia."

"Great idea!" said Ellie. "Why don't we make a start at my house tomorrow?"

"Perfect," said Jamila. "I hope Sienna will like her surprise party."

"She'll love it," said Katie. "We just need to be careful we don't let slip about it."

Grace nodded. "It's going to be hard to keep it secret when she gets back on Friday."

"Ready for us to go bowling with her on Saturday!" Katie grinned.

On Thursday the girls met up to make the posters for their badge work at Ellie's house. As they had juice and cookies, they chatted away about the things they'd been finding out for their World guiding badge.

"I found out that Brownies in Austria are called *Wichtel*," said Jamila, munching on a cookie; "and that the ones in Luxembourg are called *Wüchtelchen*, which is nearly the same!"

"In Malta the Brownies are called Brownies!" Ellie giggled.

"You know in some countries where they don't speak English, they even have English-speaking units of Brownies and Guides – just like ours," said Katie.

"I've got an even better fact," said Grace. "Sienna said that there are Guides in Australia called Lone Guides, who keep in touch with their Leaders on the internet."

"Why?" asked Charlie.

"Well, Sienna told us that there are places in Australia that are really remote," said Grace.

"She said that some children live so far away from towns that they can't even get to school," Katie added.

"How cool is that!" Ellie grinned at the thought. "Imagine not ever having to go to school!"

"Yeah – but imagine not having any friends to play with, either," said Charlie. "That would be awful."

"Sienna said that the children have to do school work anyway," Grace explained.

"They do it online," added Katie.

"Awesome!" said Charlie.

"But if they don't live near a school, then they can't be near a Guide unit, either," exclaimed Jamila. "That's terrible!"

The others agreed with her.

"Well, it's cool that those girls can be Lone Guides," said Charlie. "But I'd really miss it if I couldn't go to Brownies every week."

"Me too!" said the others.

"I can't wait for Sienna to get back tomorrow," sighed Katie.

"But first we need to get on with these posters!" Ellie grinned. "Come on!"

87

On Saturday, Charlie, Ellie and Jamila met up with Katie, Grace and Sienna at the bowling alley.

"How was your trip?" asked Charlie, as she keyed their names into their lane's computer.

"It was fantastic!" said Sienna, grinning. "There was so much to see – look!"

She took out her digital camera and showed them some of the photos she'd taken of castles and other places she'd visited.

"Wow!" sighed Ellie, tying the laces on her bowling shoes. "You've been busy!"

"Come on," said Katie. "We'd better get going or I won't get the chance to beat all of you!"

"You wish!" laughed Sienna. "Hey, Jamila, you go first!"

In fact, it was Ellie who had the highest score at the end of the evening.

"That was really good fun," sighed Grace, as the six friends tucked into a pizza. They were all sitting in the kitchen at Grace and Katie's house, exhausted after the bowling because they'd giggled so much.

"So," said Sienna, "how are you getting on with completing your challenges for the World guiding badge?"

"Well, we've done two so far," said Katie. "We've made a friendship circle and some posters all about Australia."

"And we're all going to write a postcard to your Guide unit," Jamila pointed out. "So that makes three."

"And you're going to show us how to make

Lamingtons," Ellie added, "so that's four."

"So we just need one more," said Grace.

"I know," said Sienna, grinning. "How about I teach you an Australian Guide song? There's a great one called 'The Kookaburra Song'!"

"Brilliant!" said Jamila. "What's a kookaburra?"

"Its an Australian bird," Sienna explained. "An Australian Guide wrote a song about it years ago. We always sing it at camp."

"How does it go?" asked Grace.

"I'll teach you," Sienna replied, "but will you do something for me?"

"What?" asked Jamila.

"Well, if I'm going to get my World guiding badge too," said Sienna, "then I need

you to teach me one of your songs."

"How about 'London's Burning'?" said
Katie.

"Yes!" the others agreed.

"Great," said Sienna. "OK, I'll sing the
first verse of 'Kookaburra' on my own and
then you sing it with me…"

They listened as Sienna sang. Then Ellie
asked, "Do we have to sing it exactly like you,
with an Australian accent and everything?"

The others burst out laughing.

"Just because it's an Australian song doesn't
mean you have to *sound* Australian!" Jamila
replied.

"Oh!" Ellie giggled.

"Come on," said Sienna, smiling. "Let's
sing it together!"

On Sunday, Jamila's mum and dad offered to take the girls to Badenbridge Zoo.

"My brothers are on Cub camp," Jamila explained, "so not only are they out of my hair, but there's plenty of room in the car too!"

As soon as the girls arrived at the zoo, they shot off to the gorilla pen. It was Charlie's favourite place to visit in the whole of Badenbridge Zoo.

"Hey – look at the baby one!" she said, running over to one of the huge windows at the side of the pen.

"Isn't she cute," said Sienna, squashing her nose up against the glass.

"Aww!" cried all the girls as the baby gorilla looked at them with her huge eyes.

"Do you have a zoo near where you live?" Jamila asked Sienna.

"Yes – in Melbourne." Sienna grinned. "They've got the cutest koalas and wombats. Tell you what, when you girls all come over to Australia one day, I'll take you there!"

"Cool!" all the friends replied at once.

The six girls walked around the zoo for

hours with Jamila's mum and dad. There was so much to see and do!

"Come on," said Jamila's mum, looking at her watch. "Is anyone else as hungry as I am?"

"Me!" all the friends called out.

"Well, let's have our picnic then!"

After a delicious lunch, the friends had a bit more time to wander around before Jamila's parents finally persuaded them that it was time to go home.

"We've seen all the animals now," said Jamila's dad, walking them to the car. "We've even seen the reptiles and the insects!"

"I can't believe that you really have spiders the size of a hat in Australia!" said Ellie, shivering at the thought.

"I know!" Sienna laughed, climbing into the car. "My dad says you wouldn't want to find one in the loo!"

All the girls burst out laughing.

"That was a great day, Dad," said Jamila.

"Yes," added Charlie. "Thanks so much for taking us."

"Yes, thanks," the other girls said as well.

Jamila's dad smiled. "Glad you could all come. Everyone got their seat belts fastened? Right, let's go!"

"I can't stop yawning," said Charlie, after school the next day.

All the girls had met up at Katie and Grace's house for tea.

"Well, you'd better not be too tired for tomorrow night," warned Ellie.

"What's happening tomorrow night?" Sienna wondered.

"It's the par—" Ellie started to say, but Katie quickly interrupted her.

"It's Brownies!" Katie said, shooting Ellie a look. She'd almost let it slip about Sienna's surprise party!

"So what's for tea?" said Charlie, quickly trying to get the conversation back on track.

"Lamingtons!" said Sienna.

"You've made some more Lamingtons?" Ellie said, licking her lips and thinking about the delicious Australian cakes.

"Not yet," said Sienna. "*We're* going to make some more Lamingtons – for your World guiding badge. Mum and I have been shopping today to get all the ingredients."

"Cool! Can we make some extra ones for Brownies tomorrow?" Grace asked, quickly adding, "I was just thinking that it would be great if the other Brownies could try them too – they're so delicious!"

"Good idea!" said Charlie, winking at her friend. Now they'd have extra cakes to take to the party!

"OK," said Sienna, smiling. "Mum will be here in a minute to help us, but shall we get started?" she asked, pointing to the kitchen worktop where all the ingredients were ready.

"Absolutely," Jamila said, pushing up her sleeves. "Let's get baking!"

Chapter 9

Charlie, Ellie and Jamila made sure that they arrived at Brownies early the next night so they could check on the sunflowers and then help to decorate the hall. Everyone put out the work they had been doing for their World guiding badge, and hung up the banners and the Brownie friendship circles that they had made a few weeks before. Ellie also handed the extra posters she and her best friends had made over to Vicky.

"Those are wonderful, girls!" Vicky said. "Thank you. Now, why don't you all help put out our feast on the table?"

All the Brownies had brought delicious

food from around the world for the party.

"Yum," said Charlie. She looked at her watch. "Quick – they'll be here in a minute!"

For the first and only time ever, Katie and Grace made sure that they were a little bit late for Brownies so that they could be certain all the others had arrived.

"You go first," said a grinning Grace, letting Sienna go ahead of her.

"What do you think we'll do tonight?" asked Sienna, pushing open the hall door. She looked up and gazed around, open-mouthed.

"Surprise!" screamed all the Brownies when they saw their Australian friend.

"What's going on?" Sienna asked, smiling broadly as she read the "Farewell, Sienna!"

banner hanging across the back wall of the hall. "You girls never told me about this!"

"That's because it was a surprise," Charlie laughed.

"Come on," said Vicky. "We've got a couple of things to do in the Brownie Ring before the party can begin!"

The first thing the Brownies had to do was pack their parcel for the 2nd Olave Valley Guides. They had a big empty box, ready to be filled.

One by one, the Brownies presented their gifts. They included:

* Lots of photographs of Badenbridge and the Brownies
* A Brownie T-shirt
* A selection of Brownie badges
* Some Brownie books
* Ideas for Brownie celebration food
* Some bookmarks and other crafts
* Some stamps
* Postcards - one from each of the Brownies

"Wow!" said Charlie, looking into the box.

"My friends at Guides are going to be so excited when they open this!" exclaimed Sienna when she saw everything they were sending.

"Good!" said Vicky. "We'll post this off tomorrow."

"Right," said Sam, "the second thing we need to do is read our email!"

"You mean we've had an email from Sienna's Guide unit already?" exclaimed Caitlin.

"Yessss!" all the Brownies cried.

"I can't wait to hear what they've been up to while I've been away," Sienna said.

"This is brilliant," said Ellie, hugging her new friend.

All the Brownies sat up to hear what the 2nd Olave Valley Guides had said.

Dear First Badenbridge Brownies,

It was really great to get your email all the way from the United Kingdom. We loved hearing about the new guiding friends that our own Guide, Sienna, has made since she's been with you.

It sounds like you have just as much fun with your Challenges and Adventures as we do in Australia. The film you sent us was terrific and it has inspired us to make a film too. When we've finished it, we will email it to you!

We have Guide meetings once a week and meet in the Olave Valley Scout and Guide Hut. We've got an indoor climbing wall and an adventure area outside. Like you, we put on shows and go on outings, sometimes with the Scouts. We also have sleepovers and go on camps.

One of our Guide Leaders went to a big Girl guiding conference a couple of years ago and met some Brownies and Guides from the UK as well as Canada, New Zealand, America, and lots of African and European countries. They all sent each other postcards afterwards and now we have a postcard wall that links us with Girl guiding all around the world.

We'll write to you again soon to tell you what we've been up to. Please keep in touch with us and say hello to Sienna. We're looking forward to seeing her home soon and finding out more about the First Badenbridge Brownies!

All the Brownies in the Ring grinned and chatted excitedly about the email.

"Fancy meeting Brownies from all around the world!" exclaimed Ellie.

"How cool is that?" agreed Charlie.

"Hey, Sienna!" said Grace. "Have you been up the climbing wall?"

Sienna smiled at her cousin. "Sure!" she said. "I did it last year."

"Was it really, really scary?" asked Ashvini.

"Well, I tried it once when I was a bit younger," Sienna confessed. "I didn't like it then, so our Leader said to leave it for a while. No one has to go up the climbing wall – it's up to you. Anyway, I tried it again last year and I managed to get up to the top!"

"Wow!" exclaimed all the Brownies.

"I wish we had a climbing wall!" sighed Katie, who decided there and then that one

of her next Brownie challenges would be to
go up one.

Vicky and Sam put up their right hands
and soon the hall fell silent.

"Who's ready to party?" asked Sam.

"Me!" yelled every girl in the room.

The party was just brilliant. The Brownies
feasted on all the delicious food and drink
that everyone had brought, including
Sienna's famous Lamingtons.

"These are just so good," said Jasmine.

"They are the best!" agreed Caitlin. "Who
brought them?"

Ellie explained how Sienna had taught
the five best friends how to bake the
Australian treat.

"Well, you can make them again any

Brownie night you like," said
Ashvini, licking chocolate from
her fingers.

After the feast, the Brownies
played lots of their favourite
games as well as some games that
Sienna had taught them since she'd
been at Brownies. They began with
Hedgehogs, where you had to scrunch up in
a ball on the floor and your Sixer had to
quickly work out which Brownies belonged
to her Six without being able to see their
faces. They played it against the clock and
the quickest Sixer was the winner.

In between the games, the Brownies who
had been on Brownie Holiday or Camp
taught the other Brownies some songs they'd
learned around the camp fire. Then Sienna,
Jamila, Katie, Ellie, Charlie and Grace

performed "The Kookaburra Song" that
Sienna had taught them. Everyone enjoyed it
so much that they all joined in and sang it
too. Finally, Vicky and Sam called all the
Brownies together for Sienna's last
time in the Brownie Ring.

"This has been a happy and sad
Brownie meeting all in one,"
declared Sam. "Sienna, it's been
great fun having you with us.
We've all learned a lot about
guiding in Australia and we
hope you've enjoyed your
time with us."

"It's been really awesome," said Sienna,
grinning. "Thanks for letting me come and
join you. I've made loads of new friends."

"Yesss!" agreed all the 1st Badenbridge
Brownies, and Vicky and Sam laughed.

"OK," said Sam as the hall fell silent again. "Vicky and I have been looking around the hall at all the wonderful things you've been finding out about Brownies and Guides around the world. You've all worked incredibly hard. Has it been fun?"

"Yesss!" the Brownies replied.

"Good!" said Vicky. "We've checked everyone's projects and, because you've done so many tasks towards your badge, you've already completed your badge work. You can *all* receive your World guiding badge tonight!"

"Yay!" all the Brownies cheered at once.

One by one, the Brownies went up to be presented with their badges. The last person to go up, smart in her Australian Guide outfit, was Sienna.

"Sienna," said Sam, "we have really loved having you as part of First Badenbridge Brownies and, in honour of your visit to the United Kingdom, we'd like to present you with this special British Friendship badge as well as your World guiding badge!"

As Daisy filmed the special Brownie ceremony to send on to the 2nd Olave Valley Guides in Australia, Vicky stepped forward to shake Sienna's hand.

"Sienna's visit has reminded us that each one of you has friends who are Brownies and Guides all over the world. In fact, you've got ten million other friends to meet!" said Vicky. "Now, I think, Sienna – and all of you – deserve a special Brownie clap!"

When the clapping had stopped, Vicky and Sam announced that it was time to end the Brownie meeting.

"Oh no!" Sienna exclaimed. "It can't be over already!"

"No!" sighed all the other Brownies as well.

"Sadly, it is," said Vicky.

"We thought we'd end with a song," added Sam.

All around the room, the Brownies joined hands with Vicky, Sam and Daisy. Then they began to sing:

We're Brownie Guides,
We're Brownie Guides,
We're here to lend a hand,
To love our God and serve our Queen
and help our homes and land.
We've Brownie friends,
We've Brownie friends in north, south,
east and west,
We're joined together in our wish
to try and do our best!

Chapter 10

Next day, Ellie, Grace, Katie, Charlie and Jamila were playing together after school.

"I can't believe that Sienna's not going to be at our next Brownie meeting," said Jamila.

"It'll be weird at home without her too," said Katie.

"When did she leave?" asked Ellie.

"They went to the airport this morning," explained Grace. "But they won't actually be home until Thursday evening!"

"Do you think Sienna will tell us when she's got home?" asked Jamila.

"She said she'd email," explained Katie.

"I expect you'll hear from her soon," said Jamila, giving her friend a hug.

"Maybe we can make some more Lamingtons in her honour for Brownies next week," said Ellie.

"That sounds good!" said Katie and Grace at the same time.

"Jinx 1, 2, 3!" said the others, laughing.

Every day at school, the Brownies faithfully checked up on their sunflowers. The plants were beginning to get quite tall. So, at the next Brownie meeting, Vicky and Sam decided that they would plant them outside in the school garden.

"We can do that after we've had our Pow Wow," said Vicky, when all the Brownies were sitting in the Ring, "but first, I wondered if any of you have any news for us this week?"

Katie and Grace put up their hands.

"So you two," said Sam. "Do you both have the same news?"

They nodded. "We've had an email from Sienna!"

"What does it say?" asked Vicky.

"She says she got back just in time for Guides night," explained Grace.

"They haven't got our parcel yet," added Katie, "but she told them about it and they are going to send us a parcel too!"

All the Brownies whispered excitedly, wondering what the parcel might contain.

"And Sienna sent us a photo by email!"
said Grace. "Look!"

After handing the
photo to Vicky and
Sam, it was passed
around the Brownie
Ring for all the
Brownies to look at.

It showed Sienna with
the rest of the 2nd Olave Valley Guides
standing in front of a banner that read:

HI TO THE 1ST BADENBRIDGE BROWNIES IN THE UK!

"Wow!" exclaimed the Brownies.

"Isn't that great?" said Vicky.

"Fantastic!" agreed Sam.

"I think it's amazing that we've got

Brownie and Guide friends in Australia even though we haven't ever met them," announced Jamila.

"That's one of the things that being a Brownie is all about," said Daisy.

"I've just realized," said Grace. "We come to Brownies round the corner…"

"…and then we travel with them around the world!" finished Katie.

"Come on then," said Vicky. "Let's sing a special Brownie song in celebration."

"Yes," said Sam. "We'd better get on because we've got so many adventures to have this evening!"

"Yesss!" the Brownies said.

"Everyone join hands, in our Brownie friendship circle," said Vicky.

The 1st Badenbridge Brownies linked hands with each other.

Your Brownie hand in my Brownie hand,
And my Brownie hand in your Brownie hand.
We have Brownie friends in many lands,
Across the seven seas,
the mountains and the sands.

Another Brownie meeting had begun!

When their meeting had ended, Jamila,

Charlie, Grace, Katie and Ellie were waiting at the hall door to be collected by their parents. They were looking at the photo Sienna had sent.

"I know Sienna wasn't here for long," sighed Ellie, "but I'm really going to miss her."

"Me too," agreed Charlie.

"But it's like Vicky and Sam said – Sienna's an Australian Guide, so she's our Brownie friend too."

"A friend forever!" said all the girls at once.

Sienna's Lamington Recipe

You will need to have an adult to help you make Lamingtons. Make sure you wash your hands and wear an apron. Take great care around hot things!

Makes 15

Cake:

Melted butter, to grease
75g self-raising flour
75g plain flour
70g cornflour
6 eggs, at room temperature
215g caster sugar
1 tbsp boiling water

Icing:

300g icing sugar
35g cocoa powder
60ml milk
60ml boiling water
170g desiccated coconut

You will need:

19x29cm baking tin and baking paper for lining
sieve
mixing spoon, whisk or electric whisk
3 mixing bowls
large metal tablespoon
wire rack
tea towel
plate
2 forks

Method

1. Preheat oven to 160°C. Brush the baking tin with melted butter to lightly grease. Line the base and sides with non-stick baking paper, allowing it to overhang slightly.

2. Sift the different flours together into a large bowl. Break the eggs into the other bowl and whisk until thick and pale. Gradually add the sugar to the beaten eggs, 1 tbs at a time, whisking well after each addition until mixture is thick and sugar dissolves.

3. Sift the flour mixture over the egg mixture. Pour the boiling water down the inside edge of the bowl. Use the tablespoon to gently fold the flour and water in until just combined. Pour mixture into the prepared tin and use the back of a spoon to smooth the surface. Bake in oven for 20 minutes or until a skewer inserted into the centre comes out clean.

4. Turn the cake on to a wire rack, cover with a clean tea towel and set aside to cool. If you can bear to, leave the cake overnight! When cool, cut into 15 squares.

5. To make the chocolate icing, sift the icing sugar and cocoa powder into a mixing bowl. Add the milk and water and stir until smooth.

6. Spread the coconut over a plate. Use 2 forks to dip 1 cake square into the warm icing to coat evenly on all sides. Allow any excess icing to drip off. Now roll the cake in the coconut to coat evenly, then place on a wire rack. Repeat with the remaining cake squares. Set aside for 1 hour until icing sets. Or until you can't resist any longer!

How Ashvini got her World guiding badge!

1. Made a friendship circle of dolls.

2. Spoke to Sam and Vicky about how exciting it was to know she had Brownie friends in other countries.

3. Sent an email to her cousins in India, asking them about what they did at Brownies and telling them what she got up to with her Brownie unit.

4. Drew a picture of Pax Lodge and made it into a jigsaw.

5. Created a poster about India, and used it to tell the rest of her unit about the country and the Brownies who live there.

World guiding

How to make a Jigsaw Puzzle!

You will need:

A drawing or photograph
**A sheet of card the same size
   as your picture**
Some paper glue
A pencil
Some scissors
**A box or bag to keep the
   puzzle in when it is finished**

1. Glue the picture to the sheet of card. (Ashvini used the card from the lid of a shoe box for her jigsaw.)

2. When the glue is completely dry, turn the picture over so that you can see the back of the card.

3. With a pencil, draw jigsaw puzzle shapes on the card. You need to make sure the pieces link into each other but try not to make your shapes too complicated or fiddly to cut out! The size of the jigsaw pieces is up to you. Remember that smaller pieces will make the puzzle harder to do and bigger pieces will make it easier to solve.

4. Once you are happy with the jigsaw shapes, carefully cut them out and place them in the box or bag, ready for use!

★ **Brownie Tip:** You might want to make a copy of the picture so that it can be used for reference when someone does your puzzle. You could also write on it how many pieces there are.

Collect all the books in the series!

Brownies
Perfect Promise
Caroline Plaisted

Got it!
○

Brownies
Helping Hands
Caroline Plaisted

Got it!
○

Brownies
Sleepover Surprise
Caroline Plaisted

Got it!
○

Join the Brownies

Brownies do it all!

They do cool things to get badges like the Artist badge and the Computer badge, they have sleepovers, they make heaps of friends and have lots of fun.

Brownies are aged from seven to ten and are part of Girlguiding UK, the largest organization for girls and young women in the UK, which has around 575,000 members.

To learn more about what Brownies get up to, visit www.girlguiding.org.uk/brownies or call 0800 169 5901 to find out how you can join in the fun.